LITTLE

TiGER

RESCUE

tiger tales

5 River Road, Suite 128, Wilton, CT 06897
Published in the United States 2021
Originally published in Great Britain 2020
by the Little Tiger Group
Text copyright © 2020 Rachel Delahaye
Inside illustrations copyright © 2020 Jo Anne Davies at Artful Doodlers
Cover illustration copyright © 2020 Suzie Mason
ISBN-13: 978-1-68010-480-6
ISBN-10: 1-68010-480-2
Printed in the USA
STP/4800/0389/1220

For more insight and activities, visit us at www.tigertalesbooks.com

LITTLE
TiGER
RESCUE

by Rachel Delahaye

tiger tales

For two little tigers, Ella and Olivier

—Rachel

CONTENTS

Monkey Business

"Let's be wild monkeys!" Emma shouted, waving her arms. The children copied her, spilling their drinks on the table. Callie made a face at her best friend. Emma was supposed to be helping!

"Don't encourage them!" she pleaded. "Look at the mess!"

"We're in the jungle, Callie. What do you expect?" said Emma.

The children laughed.

"We're in the jungle, Callie. What do you expect?" Freddie repeated.

Callie tried hard not to laugh. Her silly little cousin Freddie was celebrating his fifth birthday with a party at Jungle Jump, a big new jungle-themed play center in town. Callie and Emma were there to help organize some games, but when Freddie's mom stepped outside to make a phone call, they found themselves in charge of his birthday dinner. Most of which was now on the floor.

"I think they're finished eating," said Callie.

"Great, let's go and play," said Emma, jumping up and down. "Last one to the trampolines is a stinky hippo!"

Callie looked around the room. Her heart sank. She loved trampolines, but she couldn't leave the place looking like this, could she?

"You take them, Emma," she said. "I'll catch up in a minute."

The children dashed out, and Callie began stacking the plates as quickly as she could. A member of the Jungle Jump staff entered the room with a bucket and mop.

"No, no, no. That's our job," the man said kindly, taking the plates.

"But the mess—I feel terrible about

it...," Callie read his name badge, "Luke."

"Don't worry. We're used to it," he said. "Did you enjoy the jungle-themed food?"

Callie's tummy rumbled, remembering the fruit platters that had arrived and disappeared in a flash.

"Actually, the hungry monkeys scarfed all of it before I got a chance to try it!" she said.

"Here." Luke handed her a drink carton. "Have some mango juice. You'll need the energy if you're going to chase wild animals all afternoon!"

Callie laughed and slurped the juice—it was deliciously thick and sweet.

"I'd better go and find the others

before they go totally wild," she said.

Feeling better about the messy room, Callie went off in search of the party. The play center was enormous, with many different activity zones, but eventually she found everyone. They had finished on the trampolines and were now in the Monkey Climbing Room. It had a giant climbing frame that reached all the way to the ceiling, surrounded by safety nets. Emma was swinging across high horizontal bars, while Freddie and his friends watched from below in awe.

"Can you do that, Callie?" Freddie asked.

"Callie isn't strong enough," Emma called from up high. "You need stamina, like Emma the Great."

"Emma the great … more like *big baboon!*" Callie teased.

The children laughed and started making baboon noises.

"How rude!" Emma said with pretend shock. She dropped from the bars and chased Callie around and around until they both fell on a crash mat, giggling and gasping for breath.

"Play with us! Hide-and-seek, hide-and-seek, hide-and—"

"Okay, Freddie, we get the idea!" Callie laughed. "We'll count to 20. Starting from now! One…. Two…. You'd better run…! Three…."

Freddie and his friends screamed with delight and scattered, looking for hiding spots. Callie and Emma covered their eyes and continued counting.

"They went everywhere!" Emma said, peeking through her fingers. "It'll take forever to find them."

"Let's split up," Callie suggested. "We can be like sheepdogs rounding up sheep!"

"Does everything with you always have to be about animals?" Emma sighed dramatically.

"Yep!" Callie grinned. Callie loved all animals and wanted to be a vet when she grew up. She'd already taken the vet's oath—a promise to care for animals in danger.

On the count of 20, Emma went left and Callie tiptoed right, around the base of the huge climbing frame, keeping her eyes peeled for Freddie and his friends.

The jungle decorations at the play center were amazing. There were murals on the walls, toy animals in the trees, and plants made of plastic and rubber. But where were those giggling children hiding? It didn't look as if they were in the Monkey Climbing Room anymore.

Callie started to explore the other zones. She checked the Forest Floor Trampoline Room and the swings in the

Treetop Room—but there was no sign of them. Then something caught her eye—a curtain of rubbery vines. Behind it there was a doorway, and a sign: Deep Jungle Maze. And from somewhere inside the maze, Callie heard giggling. A-ha!

"Coming to get you!" she called and ran inside.

The make-believe jungle was thicker here. Pathways wove in and around tall plastic trees and bushy ferns made from felt. There were hidden speakers with sound effects: rainfall, monkey hoots, cheeping birds. But Callie couldn't hear giggling anymore.

"Where are you?" she called, walking deeper and deeper into the jungle.

By the time she reached the center

of the maze—Explorer's Rest—Callie was totally confused. She hadn't heard another peep out of the children. In fact, she hadn't seen or heard anyone at all.

She sat down on the bench. No one would mind if she stopped for a moment of peace and quiet. Filled with a sense of calm, she listened to the toots and whoops and sounds of the jungle. Closing her eyes, she imagined what it would be like to actually be there....

A New Path

Callie was dreaming she was a jungle vet, caring for sloths and leopards, when she was woken by a sound—an ear-piercing shriek! She sat upright and rubbed her eyes.

"Freddie?" She stood up. "Freddie, is that you?"

Reeech. There it was again! *Reeech.*

The noise was harsh, like a dull scream. Was someone in trouble? Was a child lost in the maze, or maybe someone had climbed a tree and gotten stuck?

"Hang on!" she called. "Stay where you are. I'll find you."

Callie went back through the winding pathways, pushing through the dense greenery, searching every twist and turn for a lost child. But there was nothing.

Reeech. Reeech.

"Where are you?" she shouted.

Just then, there was a rustle in the trees right above her head.

"Who's there?" she called, looking up. "Are you all right?"

A long-limbed shape swung down from a branch in front of her and then disappeared, quick as lightning, into the jungle behind.

What was that? Callie froze and waited. But nothing else moved. There was no sound. Not even a rustle in the trees.

"Just a cuddly toy," she said to herself. "A cuddly toy that came loose from a tree and fell down, that's all."

Callie wasn't shaken, but the strangeness of what had just happened made her more alert. She walked on, eyes and ears open. Little by little, she realized that the maze room was changing. First it was the air, which had become warmer and damp, and then it was the path. Previously it had been rubber, but now it was slightly squishy and covered in leaves. Maybe the Jungle Jump play center had some air-conditioning problems, and definitely some plumbing problems—her sandals were getting wet! She should find someone and tell them.

Suddenly, an explosion of whoops and squeaks pierced the air. It sounded like a child's toy zapper. Callie laughed, relieved that someone else was in the maze with her.

"If you're zapping me with your toy, you've got me! Look! Ugh!"

Callie stumbled backward, pretending to be hit by the zapper, but the kids didn't come out of their hiding place. She called and called, but there was no reply.

Callie decided to go back to the middle of the maze and take the quick exit path out. She should tell someone about the strange noises and the wet floor. But when she turned around, a tree was blocking her path! That definitely hadn't been there before … or had it?

Callie placed her hand on the trunk. It was rough with stringy bark that peeled away in her fingertips. Then, with a loud chorus of shrieks, the kids appeared….

Five of them ran down the tree and then up another one. They scooted to the top and flung themselves around in the branches, slipping and tumbling like gymnasts. Callie's mouth fell open. Monkeys! *Real* live monkeys!

One of them dropped down to a branch just above her and sat scratching its back. Callie remained absolutely still and tried to figure out what kind of monkey it was. It had a silky white coat and a round black face. Its limbs were long and lean.

"I think I know what you are," she said. At the sound of her voice, the monkey stopped scratching and looked at her. "You were in the *Animals of India* program I watched last week.... You're a langur!"

The langur made a squeaking noise and disappeared.

"Well, one thing is certain," Callie said to herself, placing a hand on her racing heart. "I'm not in the play center anymore!"

She looked around at the trees, and
the plants that filled every gap between
them—tumbling vines and cascading
bushes with deep pink flowers. Callie
felt the leaves and rubbed them between
her fingertips, releasing their earthy
smells.

She was half terrified and half
thrilled. How had she ended up in a real
jungle? She had been to some amazing
places before, including the Serengeti
and Antarctica, and she'd had to save a
lost animal to get home. Would it be the
same here?

Callie picked her way through the
deep jungle, watching where she put her
feet in case there were little animals on
the ground. She listened carefully, too.
Bird calls echoed in the canopy above.

It was all so magical and pretty, like a dream world. But a totally new sound made her stop dead in her tracks.

Great crashes. Trees falling to the ground. Branches snapping.

Crash, crash, crash. Like the footsteps of a giant.

Callie hid behind a tree, holding her breath as the noise grew louder. Whatever was making it was coming closer....

Then elephants appeared, stomping over everything in their path. From behind her tree, Callie could see six or seven of them, although there might be more. She stared at them in amazement. They were so close that she could see their wise little eyes and the baggy, gray-brown skin that

wrinkled under their tummies and
around their knees. They had smallish
ears, but it was the double bump on
their heads that told Callie that these
were Indian elephants. She shook her
head in disbelief. One minute she
was rounding up wild children, the
next she was in a real jungle, standing
alongside a herd of wild creatures!

Callie was mesmerized, but she had
to be careful. Elephants traveled in
families—they were protective and
loyal. If they felt threatened, they could
stampede! She had to stay completely
still. Breathing slowly to stop herself
from shaking, Callie watched as they
snapped off juicy green branches with
their trunks and put them into their
mouths.

There was a rustle behind her.
Something had moved up close. Oh, no!
Had the herd surrounded her? Was she
trapped? Slowly, Callie turned around.

The Temple Ruins

Callie didn't know who was more
frightened—herself, or the herd of deer
she had startled! She had been standing
so still that the deer hadn't even noticed
her as they stooped to nibble the plants
at her feet. Now they sprang, panicking,
in all directions. Callie only had a
few seconds to admire their attractive
markings—light brown with snow-white
spots—before they disappeared into the
trees.

Callie's heart was galloping. Luckily, it had only been deer! Next time it could be something bigger, or an animal with sharp teeth. She had to be watchful—she was in the real jungle now. And if she was here to rescue an animal, then she needed to find it. The trouble was, it was hard to find anything in such dense jungle. There were only plants and trees as far as the eye could see.

Everywhere Callie looked, it was the same. Green to the left, to the right, and even up above, where the trees created a roof of leaves, and she couldn't see the sky beyond. How was she going to pick a direction to explore when she didn't know which way was up or down! She had to make a decision.

Callie chose to go in the opposite

direction of the elephants. Although they were amazing, she didn't want to disturb them, and it would be safer to stay away from the herd.

As she walked, the bird calls echoed continuously, and Callie started to feel a little dizzy. She put one foot in front of the other, floating in and out of thoughts. She was woken from her trance by a distant roar, like the thundering of a waterfall.

She made her way toward the sound. And then she saw it—not a waterfall, but a wide, rushing river. If she followed it, maybe she would find a village and someone to talk to!

Feeling happier now, Callie continued more quickly, not caring that her feet were sinking into soggy ground right up to her ankles. Eventually she came to an area

where the plants had been cleared away
and the ground was smooth. It looked like
a place where boats might be launched into
the river, although there were none there
now. No one would be crazy enough to go
fishing when the water was so choppy. On
the other side of the clearing, a path
continued along the bank. It was clearly
marked, with two parallel lines grooved
into the forest floor. Tire marks! *It has to
lead somewhere*, Callie thought. She started
to run.

As she ran, Callie was so busy watching out for animals that she didn't notice the surface beneath her feet changed, and she tripped.

Concentrate, Callie! she told herself. *You don't want to fall down or twist your ankle.*

She looked at the ground. The tire tracks were gone! Turning around, she saw that a few steps back they curved sharply to the left, away from the river. She'd run straight ahead without noticing! Callie kicked aside the leaves and soil to see what had made her trip. Stone! Stone slabs like stepping stones, which formed a new path. Who would lay stepping stones in a jungle?

The path was slippery with moss and wet plants, and the way ahead was thick with bushes. Obviously, it hadn't been used for a long time.... But Callie was intrigued. She had to know what was inside the overgrowth!

Callie fought her way through the bushes until she reached a big stone courtyard. It was surrounded by rundown buildings. Some had flat roofs, while others were domed. Some had no roofs at all. Thick vines wrapped themselves around pillars and columns like the tentacles of a giant monster. The entire place looked ancient and forgotten. As if the forest had taken the land back for itself. Callie felt as if she had stumbled across a secret.

"A temple," she gasped. "An ancient temple on the banks of the river!"

It was enchanting. The air was still
and thick with moisture, and even
though it was right next to the roaring
river, it seemed perfectly tranquil.
There was no sound within the temple
grounds, except for the dripping of
water and Callie's footsteps as they
scuffed on the stone, then—

Mrrrrow.

It was a tiny sound, but Callie heard it. It sounded like a cat's meow. Callie turned in circles, hoping to see what had made it.

"Where are you, kitty?" she called.

Mew. Mrrrrow.

There was something about the cry—so tiny and desperate. Could it be an animal that needed her help? Surely cats weren't supposed to be in the jungle. Callie had to find out if it was okay. But where was it? She made her way through the fallen walls and rocks, searching for a sign of life. The cry came again, and Callie stopped and listened. Over there!

The mewing echoed from inside a temple room that was still standing, unharmed by time or creeping vines. It was dark inside, and Callie hesitated in the doorway. She didn't want to scare the cat away. Tiptoeing as carefully as she could, she stepped forward and peered into the gloom. It took time for her eyes to adjust, but when they did, her mouth dropped open.

The cat was there, but not the kind of cat she was expecting.

"What are you doing here all alone, little tiger?"

The Little Prince

The tiger cub jumped up. It stood and wobbled a bit before padding toward Callie clumsily on giant, fluffy paws.

"You're definitely meant to be in the jungle," said Callie, laughing to herself. "But it looks as if you're desperate for some company!"

Callie stared at the creature, amazed. The tiger cub was one of the most beautiful animals she'd ever seen. But even though she wanted to pick the fluff-ball up, she knew she'd be in danger if the mother tiger was nearby. "Wait here, little one."

Callie ran back outside and took a good, careful look around the ruins. She strained her eyes and ears for the sign of another creature, but there was nothing. Just the rush of the river on one side, the sound of the jungle birds on the other, and the rustle of leaves above. She waited and waited, but no tiger came. Something brushed against her leg, and Callie jumped back.

"Oh, it's you!" she said. The little tiger drew back its puffy, whiskery muzzle and mewed. "I guess we should introduce ourselves. My name is Callie."

The tiger seemed to like the sound of her

voice. It pricked
up its ears and
then nuzzled
against her shin.
Callie crouched
down and rubbed the
cub's back. It was bony.
She frowned. Wild animals
were usually leaner than domestic ones,
but this tiger was very thin.

Although it needed food, the cub was
confident. It kept rubbing its face against
Callie's hand, looking for contact. Callie
was more than happy to give the little tiger
some attention. She thought of the
direction she'd gone in because of the
elephant herd, and how that had helped
her find the river. Then how she had
strayed off the path and into the temple

grounds. Everything had led her here, to this tiny, lonely tiger.

"I've got a feeling I was sent here to find you," Callie said. "And take care of you!"

The tiger mewed and rubbed the top of its head against Callie's knee. *Just like a cat*, she thought. In fact, the cub was about the same size as Patches, Emma's cat. But Patches wasn't this colorful! The tiger's rich orange coat was the color of a summer sunset, and its tummy was white as snow.

It was striped all over with beautiful, black wavy lines.

Callie took the cub's face in her hands.

It was a sweet face. Fluffy, with two dark-rimmed green eyes, round as buttons.

"You're a Bengal," Callie said, examining the tiger closely. "A royal Bengal tiger."

Callie knew all about Bengals. Two years ago, she'd been given a Wild Jungle Fund adoption for her birthday. Her adopted animal was an abandoned Bengal tiger cub named Durja, who had been taken in by a local sanctuary. They sent her letters and photo updates of Durja every month, showing how the cub was growing. Callie had pinned them one by one to her bedroom wall—the perfect guide to a cub's progress! She thought back to the timeline of Durja's growth and looked at the cub in front of her.

"From your size, I guess you must be about two months old," she said, tickling the cub behind the ear. "And you definitely need some care and attention. Luckily for you, I'm going to be a vet when I grow up. I've already made a promise to keep animals safe whenever I can."

At that moment, the cub leaped up and placed both paws on Callie's knees. But it was weak, and it fell backward. Callie saw from its underside that it was a boy.

"You may be a little thing now, but I'm going to make sure you grow up to be king of the jungle!" Callie said. The cub sprang back to his feet. "King of the jungle. You like the sound of that, huh?" Callie tapped her chin.

She laughed as the tiger rolled over again on the wet ground. "Though right now you're more like a clown than a king!"

"Come here," she said, pulling him close. "You need a strong name for when you become king. Something majestic…. I know! There's a famous Indian palace called the Taj Mahal, which means crown of palaces. Taj means crown—it's perfect! Now all we need is a crowning ceremony for Taj, the crown prince!"

Callie skipped over to a nearby bush that was bursting with fragrant star-shaped flowers. "Mmm, smells like Mom's candle at home," she said, inhaling the honey scent. "But right now, the best thing about this plant is these stems!"

Callie gathered a handful of the
stringy stems and wound them around
and around each other, forming a
thick, woven circle. A jungle crown.

"Taj, come and be crowned!"

But the tiger cub wasn't interested.
He was chasing every insect that flew
past, leaping and bouncing on his
wobbly legs. Taj would never stay
still long enough to wear a crown,
so Callie popped it on her own head
to keep it safe. Then she sat on a
fallen stone boulder and watched
the cub play for a while. The poor
little thing was so thin, but his
happy nature kept him going.
Boing, boing! He was like a bouncy
ball!

When Taj got tired of chasing tiny flies, he jumped into Callie's lap. He saw the jasmine crown on her head and reached up with a giant paw to try and knock it off, like a naughty child.

"Uh-uh." Callie shook her head so the crown wobbled, teasing the tiger even more.

Taj stood on his hind legs and rested both feet on Callie's forehead, then with one swipe, he knocked the crown off her head. Callie reached to the ground to get it, but with a face full of furry tiger tummy, she rolled backward and fell off the stone. It was so funny that she couldn't stop laughing.

"Yuck, you're slobbering on me!" she said, feeling wet splats on her head.

Then there was more wet. Not

slobber, but rain. Heavy drops of it. The drumming grew louder on the canopy above. Then the rainwater began to fall right through it, pouring onto their heads. It was as if the sky had gathered up all the water in the world and was dropping it down upon them.

"Uh-oh, Taj," she said. "I think we're about to get very wet."

Monsoon!

It poured and poured—Callie had never seen anything like it before! The leaves in the trees bent under the weight of the big, warm drops, and the water tumbled down on top of Callie and Taj. *Just like a monsoon*, Callie thought. *Hang on....*

"It *is* a monsoon!" she cried. "The rainy season. Of course! Quick, Taj, we need to get inside! This might go on for a while."

Callie was already soaked through

by the time she reached the temple
room. She called for Taj, who was still
standing in the middle of the stone
courtyard, drenched. With his fur wet
and flattened, the cub looked even
thinner than before. Poor little thing!

"What are you doing? A prince
shouldn't stand in the rain!" Callie
called, crouching down in the
doorway. "Come here, little one!"

Taj looked up at the sound
of her voice and ran right
into Callie's arms.
Then he shook
his coat,
spraying
droplets
all over
her.

"Thanks, your highness," she laughed.

As rainwater began to pool in the doorway, they retreated into the dry temple room. There was nothing for them to do now but play until the monsoon shower eased. Callie gave Taj plenty of cuddles and scuttled her hand across the floor, allowing him to pounce on it. Occasionally, he gripped her hand between his teeth. It tickled most of the time, but when the cub got overexcited, his bite got harder.

Callie yelped. Taj bounced back, not realizing he'd nibbled her thumb a little too hard. Callie would have to be more careful. Cuts and bites could get infected, and there wasn't any medical equipment nearby.

"Maybe we should play a game with no

teeth," she said. "How about hide-and-seek? I'll hide—you find me."

Callie hid behind a boulder in the center of the room, and Taj followed her.

"No, no, no. You stay here." She sat Taj down facing one way, then ran off in the other direction and hid behind a pillar. "Taj, come!"

She waited for him to come, trying not to giggle as she imagined him sniffing her out. When he found her, she praised him with a lot of back rubs.

"Good job, Taj. Good job for finding me. Now try again."

Callie sat behind a stone seat. "Taj, come!"

He came padding along quickly this time and hopped into her lap. As he nuzzled against her neck, Callie felt ridiculously happy. She'd never dreamed she would be close to a wild tiger—now she was playing hide-and-seek with one! Taj was the cutest playmate. And he was smart, too. After a few tries, Callie was certain that the cub actually understood her when she said, "Taj, come."

"You are a clever little prince," she said, giving his ears a good scratch. She noticed their extraordinary markings. The fronts of his ears were orange and fluffy, but the backs were black with a single white spot in the center of each one. "You're full of surprises, aren't you?"

Outside, the rain was still falling, and the water in the doorway was now creeping into the room. Maybe there was a different way out, or another room they could move to. Callie searched the far end of the temple. It was dry, except for a crack in the ceiling. It let in raindrops, but a shaft of light also shone through, and Callie saw that there were paw prints in the dust—a lot of them. Some looked the same size as Taj's, and some were bigger. There was also a large bedding area of matted leaves…. This temple wasn't just a shelter. It was a tiger's den.

"At some point, you must have had brothers and sisters here with you," Callie said. "And a mom."

She looked back at the doorway. The

courtyard outside was now flooded, and water was moving in fast. Callie realized what had happened.

"After the last big rainfall, your mom must have been worried that the den would flood. Maybe she moved her litter … but you got left behind." Callie was overcome with emotion. She ran to Taj and took him in her arms. "How could anyone forget you?"

Then as suddenly as it had started, the rain stopped. After the splattering and drumming, the silence was strange. The light outside grew brighter, and the birdsong started again. But in monsoon season, Callie knew that the rain could come at any time. She placed Taj on the ground next to her.

"Your mom was right. The river is so

close, and the ground is already soaked. If it rains again soon, the water will fill this room. We need to go."

Callie took a step toward the doorway and froze. Blocking their exit was an enormous snake. It was gray-brown with white stripes. Its body was as thick as a baseball bat and longer than a jump rope. Taj ran ahead, unaware.

"Taj!" Callie called. But the snake had seen him. It began to uncoil its body. It raised its head and pulled itself up so it stood tall in front of them. "Come, Taj! Come here!"

Taj turned and ran back to her, but Callie couldn't take any more chances. She picked up the cub. Then she stamped her feet, hoping the vibrations would scare the snake away.

Instead, the alarmed snake raised its head even higher and fanned out its neck to form a hood. In the *Animals of India* program Callie had seen, this snake was the star. It was a cobra, one of the most venomous snakes in the land. And it wasn't going anywhere.

River High

The cobra watched her, swaying its body every time Callie moved. It was so big that it could lurch forward and bite her if it wanted to, but for now, it was just keeping her in its sights.

Callie was terrified. She knew snakes only attacked if they thought they were in danger—it was making itself big to scare her away—but there was nowhere to go. And if the rain came again, it would push the snake farther into the temple room with them. Taj wriggled and writhed in her arms. If he got loose and upset the cobra....

There was no choice—Callie would have to scare off the snake. Gulping back fear, she stamped closer. Then closer again. But the snake jerked its head forward, making a rasping sound. A warning. To go any closer would be foolish. There was only one other thing to do—she would have to distract it.

Wedging Taj tightly under one arm, Callie took the jasmine crown from her head and danced it in the air, looping it from side to side in front of the cobra. The snake fixated on it with its blank, beady eyes. It was bristling. Its tongue flicked in and out. Callie's heart rattled. It was now or never.

She waved the crown in the air again, closer and closer, and then she threw it at the snake. It hit the side of its neck. Not hard, but hard enough to make the snake twist around. The crown bounced off its body, and the cobra darted after it as it skidded across the floor. Callie ran as fast as she could. Past the thick coils of the beast, and out into the open.

Wading through the huge monsoon puddles as deep as wading pools, she didn't stop until she reached the opposite side of the stone courtyard. She looked behind her.

The snake hadn't followed. Phew! Callie relaxed and breathed deeply, and Taj leaped from her loosened grip.

"Okay, Taj, you can walk now, but we need to watch out. The monsoon rain has probably flooded a lot of animals' nests. There could be plenty more snakes looking for shelter."

Everything was dripping with rain, and at the edge of the temple grounds where the stone met grass, Callie was shocked at how wet the ground was. It was over her sandals and up past her ankles. The ground wasn't just waterlogged—it was totally flooded! She looked up to see that the river had burst its banks, and waves of muddy brown water were spreading into the forest!

Taj had spotted something in the

murky wash and paddled out toward it.
Callie ran after him.

"What are you doing?" she panted.
"We're wet enough!"

But Taj was toying with a fish that
had been washed up on the bank. He
was at the age when he could start to
eat meat, just like Durja had done at
two months old. This fish would be
something to build up his strength.
Who knew when food would come
along again this easily?

Callie grabbed the fish with both hands
and ran backward to drier land. Taj
followed, captivated by the silvery object.
Callie held out the fish and the cub licked
it, making funny faces as his tongue
struggled with the scaly texture. Callie
tried not to laugh in case it turned him off.

As Taj grew more confident with the fish, he started to snap at it with his little teeth. After his mother's milk, it would be a very funny flavor, but the cub didn't seem to mind. He wolfed down little mouthfuls, stopping only to lick his chops and whiskers.

"You're growing up fast, little prince," Callie said. "Your mom would be proud of you."

But where was his mother? She must be worried about her lost cub.

"That's why I'm here!" she said to herself. Yes, that's why she was a million miles away from her own home. She had to help this little tiger cub find his mother.

She gazed at the cub. "Eat every last piece, Taj. We're going on a journey, and you're going to need all your strength!"

Callie remembered what Luke had said—about needing energy to take care of all those kids. If only she could find something to boost *her* energy, she'd be able to take care of Taj better.

She looked around and saw Taj loping back toward the river. He was farther out than he'd been before and dangerously close to the full force of the river. Tigers could swim, but not necessarily in a fast-flowing river flooded with monsoon rain.

Taj may have been weak, but he was
fearless. He was running deeper into the
murky floods, right up to his tummy.
Callie ran after him, splashing though the
water as fast as she could. But Taj thought
it was a game and hurled himself
backward into the waves that rippled over
the ground and sucked back into the river.

"Stop! It's too dangerous!" Callie called.

Taj seemed to understand the tone of her voice and stood still, waiting for her. But before Callie could reach him, he was knocked off his feet by a rush of water. The muddy wave returned to the river, taking Taj with it.

Callie heard a last, desperate mew before he was gone, out of sight.

The Rickety Bridge

Callie plunged into the river. The water was warm, but it still took her breath away, and the undercurrents spun her around and around. She kicked her legs to stay upright, using her arms to keep her body facing the right way. She had so little energy, but she couldn't give up. She had to get down the river as fast as possible after Taj. Where was he?

It was hard to see anything with so much debris. Old tree trunks, branches, and twigs uprooted by the monsoon bobbed alongside her, blocking her view. *They were floating….* Yes! Callie grabbed hold of a drifting log and wrapped her arms around it. Now she could keep her head above water and rest her arms and legs.

Callie had seen enough wildlife documentaries to know that there might be other things in the river, too—living things, like giant catfish or even freshwater crocodiles! But she pushed the thought to the back of her mind. She had to be strong for Taj.

"Taj!" she called, but her voice seemed to go nowhere. "Taj!" she cried again.

Callie began to feel utterly helpless. She bit her lip to keep herself from crying. Being upset wouldn't help her now—she had to keep her mind sharp while she figured out what to do. She saw something bobbing in the water. It looked like a large knot of wood. It had two round bumps on top…. A crocodile!

Callie gulped and tried to steer her log float away, but her legs thrashed helplessly against the current. She got closer and closer. Then she saw—they weren't crocodile eyes. They were tiny tiger ears. It was Taj!

The cub was struggling to keep his head above water, and Callie was still too far away to save him if he went under…. More determined than ever, she kicked her feet hard, but no amount of determination could fight the fast-flowing river.

Just when Callie thought she might

never catch up, Taj was suddenly
sucked over to the far side of the river,
where the water was moving more
slowly. There must have been shallows
or rocks beneath the surface, breaking
its speed. Yes! This was her chance.

Callie was swept closer to the cub.
She could see him clearly now. She
couldn't hear his mews above the noise
of the river, but she could see his
mouth opening and closing, revealing
little fangs. He was turning slowly
on the spot. The different speeds of
the water currents crashed together,
creating a gentle whirlpool. As he
turned, Taj spotted her, and his eyes
widened.

Mew. Mew.

"Yes, Taj. It's me. Hang on!"

Callie was still traveling in the fast
stretch of water. There was a danger
she would whoosh right past him if she
didn't time it right. If that happened,
they would be separated forever. She
carefully let go of the log with one hand
and reached out toward Taj as far as
she could. She was getting close. Closer.
Three, two, one … *stretch.*

Callie's fingers met damp fur. She gripped Taj and yanked him into the fast-flowing stream alongside her. Then she pulled him out of the water and on top of the log. The little cub was shaking like a leaf.

"I've got you. I've got you," she soothed. But the river still had them both, and she didn't know where it was taking them. Now it was only going to get faster—the monsoon showers had started again.

The raindrops made the water dance around them. It drummed and crackled. And then, out of nowhere came a mighty roar, like a soccer stadium cheering a goal. Callie peered through the rain. The water up ahead was white and foaming. Rapids!

This was bad. There might be big rocks breaking up the water, or maybe even a waterfall! Callie felt panic rise in her throat. They had to get out of there—fast. She looked around for something they could cling to, but there was nothing. The rain eased, and in the fine spray at the start of the rapids, she spotted a bridge.

It was a living bridge. Branches and vines had been woven and bonded together. Fresh vines trailed across it, some tumbling into the waters below. If she could grab hold of them in time, she might be able to climb up. But did she have the stamina? It had been so long since she'd eaten. She was using every last ounce of energy just keeping the log from rolling—keeping

Taj upright and safe. But she had to try. This was their only chance.

Carefully, Callie lined herself up with the center of the bridge, where the vines touched the water.

"You're going to have to do some stretching now, Taj," she said. "Just like when you knocked the crown off my head, remember? I know you can do it." Taj looked at her with his round green eyes, and she tried to smile.

They were seconds from the bridge. Callie was still holding on to the log with one hand. With the other, she grabbed Taj by the scruff of his neck and raised him as high as she could in the air. Her arm trembled with the effort. *This is it*, she thought. *Time to be strong.*

Just before they slipped under the

bridge, Callie let go of the log and
snatched at the vines with her free hand,
quickly wrapping her fingers tightly
around a slippery wood stem. In the other
hand, Taj struggled, terrified.

"Go!" she shouted through gritted
teeth.

Callie swung the cub upward. Taj
reached up and hooked a claw in
the vine above. The rest of his body
dangled unsteadily above her.

"You can do it!" she called as Taj's back claws found footholds. He scrambled to the top.

"Wonderful!" Callie cried. "Great job."

She was still holding tightly to the bottom of the vine. Although her arms hurt, Taj's success filled her with joy. The little tiger looked at her and mewed.

"I'm coming, bossy prince!" she said.

Callie gulped down a big breath of air and swung her legs up, hooking her feet through a loop of vines. From there, she pulled her top half upward and heaved herself onto the bridge.

They had made it!

Copycat

Callie lay on her back on the walkway, catching her breath. She closed her eyes and listened to the roar of the rapids below.

"I think we could have done without that adventure!" she said, rubbing water from her eyes. She sat up and looked around. Where was Taj?

There was a furious flapping on the other side of the river as some birds shot out of a bush, squawking with alarm. A little tiger cub crawled out from underneath it.

"Chasing birds? You naughty cat! Come on, let's head back." But Taj was busy sniffing the ground.

Maybe the cub knew something she didn't. Maybe he had caught the scent of his family.... Watching her feet on the slippery vines, Callie crossed the old bridge. She watched and waited to see where Taj's nose would lead him.... The tiger edged forward slowly, one foot after another. Then he pounced! A lizard shot between his legs and ran into the undergrowth.

"So much for keeping your mind on the job, Taj!" Callie laughed. "We're supposed to be looking for your mom, not lizards! But first...."

First, before they did anything else, she planned on giving the cub a big hug. She wanted to hold him tightly and keep him safe, just for a moment. It looked as if Taj had the same idea! As soon as Callie bent down to pick him up, he jumped into her arms and licked her face. His tongue was as rough as sandpaper.

"You'll lick my skin off if you give me any more kisses!" Callie laughed.

Then her tummy let out a long, low moan. Startled, Taj jumped backward and fell over.

"Ha ha! It's just my tummy, silly. I don't think I can survive any more adventures without food. There must be something around here I can eat. A-ha, what's that?"

Callie had spotted a wide umbrella-shaped tree. Oval orangey fruits hung in

clusters at the top, like seed
pods. The tree's V-shaped
branches made it easy to
climb, but just as Callie
was about to pull herself
into the branches, she saw
a monkey sitting farther up.

Then—ow!—something
hard fell on Callie's head.
A fruit from the tree, now
slightly squished, rolled
at her feet. Callie picked
it up, peeled away the
skin, and brought it to
her nose. She sniffed. *Hmm*,
she knew that smell. It was
sweet and wholesome, just
like the juice Luke had
given her. Mango!

73

There was a rustle in the leaves above, and another mango tumbled down. This one was greener, and certainly not ripe enough to fall off a tree by itself. Callie looked up to see the silvery langur was now awake and peering down at her with interest.

"Thanks, monkey," Callie said a little nervously. Were langurs aggressive? She couldn't remember.... It watched her intensely, as if it was waiting for something.

Callie bit into her juicy mango and made *mmmm* sounds to show it was delicious. The langur listened, head to one side. Then it reached up and twisted another mango from its stalk and carefully dropped it at her side. Callie clapped with joy. She peeled it and bit into the sweet flesh.

"Yes! Delicious! I'm going to call you Mango. Mango the monkey!"

Mango liked the cheering and clapping and jumped up and down on his branch. Callie jumped up and down, too. Then Mango clapped. Callie was now full of fruit sugars and juice, and she could feel her energy returning. This monkey wanted to play—what an experience it would be!

"Hide-and-seek with a tiger, and now copycat with a monkey!" she laughed.

Callie and Mango played copycat for a long time, and the only real cat involved —Taj—danced at Callie's feet, enjoying the excitement.

But Mango's mood suddenly changed. Callie saw it in his face. He kept turning away. Then he began shrieking and barking—a noise that cut right through her.

What did I do wrong? Callie wondered. She backed away, scared about what Mango might do. But the monkey, baring his teeth, was pointing at something in the distance. He became more and more upset, slapping the branches and then pointing over and over again.

"You're warning me about something," Callie said. Chills shot up her spine.

There was danger coming—she sensed it. She grabbed Taj and pushed him up the tree. He dug his claws into the bark and scrambled higher. Then Callie pulled herself up onto the lower branch, arms still sore. The monkey had moved to the top of the tree, so Callie climbed higher.

From her lookout, she spotted something moving through the trees. Tails—striped and thick as rope. Then she saw the bodies they were attached to…. Five animals with sleek orange and black coats, one large and four smaller. There was no mistaking what they were: beautiful Bengal tigers.

"Taj, could it be…?" Callie started. But her little cub had already run back down the tree, head first, graceful and sure. Callie followed behind clumsily, slipping on the last branch and falling to the ground on her backside. There was a shriek.

"Are you laughing at me?" Callie asked. But the monkey was still pointing and making a racket. "It's all right, Mango. That's Taj's family."

Taj ran ahead, and Callie hid behind the mango tree. She was tingling with excitement! She was about to see a happy ending—although she wished that Mango would be quiet. He seemed more agitated than ever. Why? She looked up at the monkey's expression. He was hissing. Something was wrong.

Callie looked at Taj, who had stopped,
his fur bristling. Then she looked at
the silhouettes of the tigers. They were
much bigger than him—even the small
ones. They were six months old, maybe.
Or even a year.

This wasn't Taj's family. And Taj
knew it. He shivered all over.

An Ambush of Tigers

"Taj!" she whispered, trying to get his attention.

Taj stopped and turned.

"That's right, Taj. Come!" Callie coaxed.

To her relief, the cub ran back to her. Callie pulled him into her arms and darted back behind the mango tree. If this side of the river belonged to the tiger family in front of them, then they would automatically be Taj's rivals. Callie knew that tigers patrolled their own patches of land, and something in the easy way these giants moved through the forest told her that this was definitely *their* territory. Rival tigers might see them as enemies. They were in great danger.

She heard the crack of paws on small twigs. The tigers were approaching. Callie peered around the tree trunk.

The tigers weren't far away. They sniffed the air with interest.

Was it better to stay still and be found, or run and be seen? Either way, if the tigers saw them, there'd be no escape. She gripped Taj even tighter and watched and waited, hoping they'd leave. But the mother moved ahead of her cubs, closer and closer. The tigress was huge! She had a wide face with big, almond-shaped eyes, and her coat was as luxurious as velvet. It slid smoothly over her giant muscles as she ran—it was a stunning sight. But she was running! *Running!*

There was no time to climb the tree—and besides, tigers were much better climbers than she was. Callie's only chance was to sprint to the bridge and get to the other side of the river, back into Taj's territory.

With Taj tight in her grip, she waited until the tigress turned to look at her cubs, and then she ran. The bridge was only a few feet away. She looked behind. They'd seen her and were picking up speed. Fear hit Callie like a block of ice. She couldn't outrun a tiger!

Taj clung to her, frightened. His claws dug into her like blades. All Callie could do

was run
like she'd
never run
before. Her
breath rasped,
and her lungs
burned as she
powered toward the
bridge.

Her feet hit the rickety walkway, and she
was so focused that she was almost on the
other side when she heard the monkey
shrieking again. She turned to see if
Mango was telling her something new....
But the tigers were still on the other side of
the bridge. They ducked and snarled and
turned in circles. What was going on?

Mango was throwing mangos at them!
The monkey was holding them back.

"Thank you, Mango!" Callie yelled to
her funny friend in the tree. She ran the
rest of the way across the bridge. She
didn't stop until they were safely back in
Taj's territory, which she knew rival tigers
wouldn't dare to enter. She collapsed to the
ground, and Taj crawled into her lap. She
petted him over and over until his

panicked breathing calmed.

"We will keep looking for your family, but I think we'd better stick to this side of the river from now on. You tigers are a territorial bunch!"

While they rested, Callie found herself thinking about the trouble humans brought to nature without even realizing it. Just a simple bridge connecting two territories created problems. She had read in her Wild Jungle Fund book how villages and towns expanded as their populations grew, which meant they had to clear more precious jungle to build houses. It made the tigers' territories smaller and food more scarce, and it pushed the rival tiger families closer together, which created fights.

Callie's thoughts were disturbed by

the drumming of rain. The monsoon
showers were starting again. She
plucked a huge leaf and rolled the edges
so it collected water in the middle. She
gulped some down and then collected
some for Taj, who lapped at it happily.

"Refreshed? Then let's go. And let's
keep away from the banks of the river.
I'm definitely not ready for another
swim!"

Callie walked into the forest, and Taj
trotted behind her obediently. The little
cub had become so used to her that he
could almost be a pet! But Callie knew
it was wrong to encourage that. Tigers
needed to be alert and careful in order
to survive. And although she had grown
to love Taj and would do anything for
him, she couldn't teach him tiger skills.

He needed to be with his own kind as soon as possible—before his mother forgot about him. If they were apart too long, she might not take him back.

Callie briefly wondered why the mother had never returned for her little cub. If she had stayed in her own territory, she couldn't be too far away. Although a mile of forest was hard to get through on foot.

"Let's go this way, little one," Callie said, clapping her hands to a happy beat. But although she wanted to sound happy, her heart was heavy. She worried what would become of her handsome tiger prince.

Trying to Belong

The full monsoon was upon them, and trekking was hard. After so much rain, the ground was like a bog. Now there was even more water, and nowhere for it to go. Callie's sandals kept getting stuck in the sticky soil. When she saw Taj swimming in a puddle in the middle of the forest floor, she decided that staying away from the river wasn't enough.

"We need to find higher ground,"

she said. "The water runs downhill, so if we're higher up, we won't be bogged down. We might even find a viewpoint."

After a steep climb, they reached a place where the land evened out—a wide, flat step in the side of the hill. There were fewer trees up there and a wide view of the forest, which stretched for miles like a giant green carpet. Streams of white birds drifted across the sky below like threads of cotton. It was breathtaking.

"Look at your home, Taj," Callie said, lifting the cub in the air. "Isn't it the most beautiful place in the world?"

Taj wriggled and mewed. He flipped from side to side in her arms. He seemed irritable.

"What's the matter—want to play? Okay, we've got time for a quick game of hide-and-seek, if you like."

But as soon as Callie put him down, Taj shot off toward a cluster of rocks farther along the ridge. He scrambled over a rock and out of sight. This wasn't like the times they'd played before. Callie followed Taj and found him on the other side of the rocks, lying in the grass. He didn't move when she arrived. He didn't even turn his head. He was watching something. He was shivering a little. He was cold. Or maybe he was scared....

"What is it, Taj?" Callie said, worriedly. Then she saw them.

Eyes. Four sets of eyes peered back at them through the grass up ahead. They were strange eyes, a little spooky.

I've seen those eyes before, Callie thought. *Who do they belong to?*

Before she could pick up Taj, the cub sprang forward and began bounding toward the unusual eyes. Callie, heart thumping, stayed absolutely still. There was nothing she could do. She bit her nails as she watched Taj get closer to the unknown creatures.

Wait a minute! The backs of Taj's ears! She saw them as he ran—black with white dots. Just like eyes. The spooky eyes weren't eyes at all but markings. Tigers' ears. He was running to greet tigers!

The four tigers in the grass heard Taj approaching and turned their heads, just as Taj pounced. He landed on top of one of them and nuzzled its neck. He wouldn't do that unless he knew them. *This must be his family!* Callie's eyes welled up as she was struck by waves of emotions. Hope, worry, sadness…. She hadn't said good-bye to her little prince.

But she couldn't get in the way now. She backed off and hid behind a rock to watch.

One of the tigers—just a cub—stood up and pawed Taj until he rolled over. Others came to investigate, and soon Taj was surrounded by cubs. They were all bigger than him, but he didn't seem scared or unsure. And they appeared to be patient with his playfulness.

If this was Taj's family, then these

cubs weren't big—Taj was small! He looked two months old, but maybe he was three or even four months old, like the others. Callie realized the truth—Taj was the runt of litter, the smallest. The one that doesn't thrive as well as the others.

In many animal species, there were runts, and they always had a harder time. Sometimes they didn't survive very long. But Taj would be okay, Callie was sure of it. He had enough spirit in him to flourish. He always seemed to find energy from nowhere! Now that he was home, he had a good chance of growing up to be a big, healthy tiger, just like his brothers and sisters.

Then Callie noticed the rise and fall of a large, striped, orange back moving

through the grass. Mom had returned.
In her mouth, she held a small animal
for the cubs to eat. This was great news!
Except for a tiny fish, Taj hadn't eaten
anything in a long time. Finally, he
could have a proper meal. Callie hoped
the tigress would let him eat first. Taj
looked back at Callie.

Go on, Callie mouthed. *Go on, Taj.*

Taj mewed at her once, and then
he walked very carefully toward his
mother. Callie covered her mouth to
stop her sobs of joy as he broke into a
run and shot between his mother's legs.
He nuzzled her soft tummy, happy to be
home. The mother dropped her kill and
roared.

Callie thought it was a roar of
triumph at having her cub back but

gasped in horror as the tigress then
batted Taj away with her huge paw. He
flew through the air and rolled into the
grass. The other, bigger cubs moved
to take their meat, leaving no room for
Taj. He tried again and again, each time
springing forward full of hope. But as
soon as he got close to the meat or his
mother, he was met with ferocious roars
that made the air shudder. The poor
cub trembled.

Callie couldn't stop the tears. He had been abandoned by his own family. If he stayed with them, he would starve.

"Come, Taj!" Callie rasped. "Come to me."

The other tigers didn't even notice Taj leave. Callie gathered the cub in her arms and backed away. She didn't know what to do. She had to save him—but how could she save him if he had no home to go to?

Home for Tigers

They walked down the hill, away from the territory that Taj was no longer a part of, back into the damp forest.

Callie didn't know how she could help the cub now, but she knew she couldn't leave him. What if he fell into the river looking for fish, or accidently ended up in another tiger's territory? He'd never survive.

"No," she said aloud, giving Taj a squeeze. "We're not parting ways until I find a way to keep you safe. I'm staying right here with you."

Taj began to talk a lot. It started as loud and gravely mews but got weaker and weaker as they went on. Callie remembered how he had immediately tried to nuzzle his mother. Was he asking for food? He must be so hungry. Being anywhere near the river during the monsoon was dangerous, but they had to go back and catch more fish, because who knew when they'd find something to eat again.

The roar of the water brought back bad memories, and Callie held Taj tightly as they approached the river. The water was spilling into the forest, but there were no silvery fish in its wake. There were only old branches and stones from the riverbed.

Callie was about to give up when floodwater flowing back toward the river revealed parallel tracks in the soggy grass beneath. The tire track path!

Wading through the water, which now went halfway up her shins, she walked on. Every now and then she stopped to let the water wash away again so she could check that she was still on the right path. She wouldn't leave it this time. Taj still mewed, desperate with hunger.

"I'm sorry, Taj, but we need to walk a little farther. Just a little bit farther."

Callie knew there had to be a reason for a track in the middle of nowhere. She had thought so the first time, and now she was determined to find out where it led.

The track wove in and around trees and seemed to go on forever. Then it turned sharply away from the river and headed into the thick forest again. Callie felt hope drain from her, but when she looked up, something white was glinting through the trees ahead.

"Let's go see what it is," she said to Taj.

The track stopped at a little parking lot. A white truck was parked there. And beyond it was a building surrounded by a high white wall. Callie crept closer to look. The wall was covered with writing and images. The paint was old and peeling away in many places, but Callie could still make out the outlines. She could see that the pictures were of tigers. Leaping tigers with big, wide grins.

"Wow! I think these people really like tigers. But we have to be sure they are good people before we ask for help."

Callie searched the area, looking for more information. Just above her she saw small slits along the wall—tiny windows. Standing on tiptoe, she peered through.

"Look, Taj, look!" Callie said, hurriedly lifting the cub so he could see through the window. As usual, Taj was too wriggly. "Okay, I'll tell you what I see. Tiger cubs. Happy little tiger cubs, just like you!"

Pressing her face to the window again, Callie watched as tiger cubs clambered over tree trunks and rope nets, playing together without a care in the world. Dotted around the enclosure were bowls of water and tons of food.

"I've got a good feeling about this place." She paused, blinking. "It's funny. I feel like I've been here before…. Come on. Let's go and say hello."

Callie walked back around to the front and stood outside the door. Above it was a sign in an alphabet Callie couldn't

read. There was one in English, too:
Shaanti Tiger Sanctuary.

"A tiger sanctuary!" Callie exclaimed.
"Taj, this is the answer we've been
looking for. These people will take care
of you and make sure you grow up to
be king of the jungle. It even looks like
a palace!" She gazed down at the cub,
scruffy from their adventure. She had a
lump in her throat. "Let's clean you up,
shall we?"

Callie raked Taj's fur with her
fingertips, smoothing
it down. Then
she walked
back into
the forest
to look for
slender

vines and white blossoms that smelled like honey. She wound them together in a circle.

"This is perfect," she said. "Now come and give me a hug good-bye."

Taj was more interested in playing with the newly made crown in her hand than giving hugs, but Callie held him tight. She took his face in her hands and looked once more into those green eyes.

Be happy, little prince.

Taj stopped still and looked at her, as if he realized that this was good-bye. Then he gave her a big, raspy lick across her face. Callie spluttered, but she didn't push him away. She knew that every last second with the cub was precious.

With a tummy full of butterflies, Callie led him to the door of the sanctuary and pressed the crown down on his head. She lay a mango stone at his feet—something for him to play with, to keep him on the doorstep—and then she pulled the bell rope.

Somewhere behind the wall she heard it tinkle, like birdsong. She gave Taj a last kiss on the top of his head and returned to the edge of the forest to hide and watch. Sitting under a nearby bush, she could see her little tiger cub on the doorstep, and her heart ached. It swelled with pride, too. At Taj for being brave. And at herself, for not giving up.

The door opened.

Callie heard a woman's voice—soft and surprised—and saw two hands reach down and gently wrap themselves around Taj's middle. He was lifted off his feet and taken in. The sanctuary door closed.

Back in the Jungle

Callie watched the door for a long time, but it didn't open again. Her tiger adventure was over.

She started to walk back down the path toward the river, feeling happy but sad, joyful but miserable. Although she knew that she would miss Taj every day, she also knew that he was in the best place now. With a tear in her eye, Callie took one last look behind her.

The *Shaanti Tiger Sanctuary*. It was

such a beautiful name.

She said the words over and over, suddenly remembering the pictures sent to her by the Wild Jungle Fund. Of a cub in an enclosure with logs and food, and a sanctuary wall with a door and a sign above it....

Of course! She knew she had seen this place before. Durja had been cared for here. Right here! Durja had grown up to be big and strong, and now Taj would, too! Callie clapped her hands for joy. Little Taj, runt of the litter and rejected by his family, would one day have a family of his very own.

With Taj safe and sound, it was time for Callie to return to her own family. But where was the path home? Maybe the answer would suddenly appear, just as it had before.

Callie stepped off the track and wandered into the undergrowth, swinging her sore arms and shaking out her legs. There was no rain now. In a patch of forest where a stream of sun had broken through the canopy, she stopped and closed her eyes. She breathed in the warm, sweet smells and listened to the calls of the birds, whooping and whistling in the treetops.... She wanted to be able to remember this, always.

Then a raucous cackle broke the silence.

Monkeys!

Callie looked up, hoping it was Mango. She'd never had the chance to thank him. With her eyes on the treetops, she didn't notice a curtain of vines hanging in front of her. She walked right into them, her arms and legs getting tangled in them instantly. Somewhere above her, the monkeys hooted.

"Laughing at me, are you? I think I preferred it when you were throwing mangoes!" she called, fighting her way out of the vines.

On the other side of them, she found herself looking at…

"Emma!" Callie gasped.

"Who was throwing mangoes?"

"What?" Callie spun around to look at

the jungle behind her. It was made of plastic, rubber, and felt. She was back!

"I said, who was throwing mangoes? Was it the kid with the red striped T-shirt? I bet it was. He's a bit of a handful…."

Just then, their birthday group ran at them, screaming. Freddie stopped at Callie's feet.

"Be scared!" he insisted. "We're jungle lions."

"Lions don't live in the jungle," Callie said, still a little confused. "*Tigers* live in the jungle!"

"Yeah, we're tigers. Now run for your lives, or we'll eat you up!"

Emma and Callie screamed with laughter and ran to the Monkey Climbing Room, with Freddie and his friends chasing them as fast as they could.

"Let's cross the monkey bars," Callie said. "It'll be harder for them to get to us if we're on the other side."

"Okay, let's go!" Emma followed Callie up to the bars and watched, astonished, as her friend flew across them. "You *do* have stamina!"

"You can say that again." Callie grinned. "I'm strong enough to do anything! Come on, let's hide in there."

The girls jumped down into the middle of a giant ball pit and covered themselves in plastic balls to hide from the tigers.

"Hurry up," said Emma, nudging Callie along. "Um…. Why is your top wet, Callie?"

"Oh, that," Callie said. "I've been in the monsoon."

Just then, an ambush of tigers pounced on top of them with shouts of "Found you! Found you!" Somewhere a whistle blew. It was the end of the play session, and the end of the party.

One by one, the party guests left, until it was just Callie, Emma, Freddie, and his mom.

"Thanks so much for helping out, girls," said Callie's aunt, smiling. "I couldn't have done it without you." She started to give Callie a hug and then stepped back. "Why are you damp?"

"She was in the moss room," Emma explained.

"What's the moss room?" Callie said.

"I don't know. A room covered in wet moss or something. You should know, Callie. You're the one who was there."

"Oh, Emma," Callie said, trying hard not to laugh. "I said I'd been in the monsoon. Why would there be a room full of moss?"

Emma's eyes widened, and she held her hand in front of her mouth. "Monsoon! Moss room!" she shrieked. The two girls laughed at her mistake all the way home.

When Callie got back to her house,
exhausted and happy, she dug into a
delicious dinner. Then she hopped
right in the bath and got into her
pajamas. It was only six o'clock, but she
was tired and ready for bed. She felt as
if every muscle in her body
was yawning.

Before she went to bed, Callie turned
on the computer in her dad's study.
She typed in the address of a website
and sat back as it opened up.

The Wild Jungle Fund website
brought back a flood of memories.
There were pictures of the jungle
filled with pretty blossoms and trees
dripping with mangoes—there were

even langurs in the branches! Snakes, too! Callie clicked through them all, remembering the smell of the rain and the warm, wet earth.

Then she clicked on the Tiger Rescue page.

It talked about how you could donate money to support local tiger sanctuaries, which rescued cubs and helped them grow into strong, healthy adults. There were photographs of big, sleek tigers being released back into the wild—the caretakers throwing flower petals at their feet as they left. It was magical! Callie felt sad that she would never get to see her own little prince walk on petals to take his place in the jungle....

There was a button for New

Arrivals, and Callie clicked on it. A
video came on—there was a webcam
inside the sanctuary! It showed a
big enclosure with climbing logs
and bowls of food. And then, right
up close to the camera, a little cub
suddenly appeared. It peered into the
camera with its bright, green button
eyes.

Taj?

The tiger cub sprung back and tilted
his head to one side. Those little ears
and twitchy whiskers—there was no
mistaking them. He licked his chops
with a big, prickly tongue and rolled
on his back with his legs in the air.

"It *is* you, it is!" Callie laughed.
"No one else could clown around
like that!"

The cub sprang to his feet and **ran** to play with his friends. He turned back and mewed, just once, before disappearing beneath a tumble of **tiger** cubs.

Callie wiped a tear from her eye. "Good luck, my little prince."

The video came to an end. Callie sighed and placed a hand on her heart. She was about to log off when she stopped, feeling a spark of excitement. She thought of adoption packs and updates and photos that arrived once a month showing the rescued cubs growing....

Callie grinned from ear to ear as a most amazing idea crept into her tired mind. In the morning, she would ask her parents to click the big red button at the bottom of the page. The one that said ADOPT NOW.

Callie crawled into bed and sighed with happiness. She would see her little prince grow up to be a king, after all.